A Basketball Cheater Caught on Tape!

The five friends focused their attention back on the TV. Ray Washington flipped a ball through the hoop and then began jogging downcourt, into a crowd of players. Suddenly, Ray was sprawled on the court clutching his ankle.

"Wow," Corey said. "It happened so fast."

"He must have stepped on it wrong," Sam added. "It was a freak accident."

But Jack wasn't so sure. A blur on the screen had caught his eye. It had been almost too quick to notice, but he knew he had seen *something*.

"Hey, Bryan," he said. "Could you play that again?"

Bryan pressed rewind on the remote control.

Jack moved closer to the screen. He watched Ray Washington jog back down the court. Once again, Ray cut through a crowd of people—and then suddenly hit the floor.

Lara squinted at the television. "What do you see, Jack?" she asked.

"I think Ray might have been tripped," Jack replied.

Look for these other
Sports Mysteries books:

#1 The Case of the Missing Pitcher

#2 The Haunted Soccer Field

#3 The Mystery of the Stolen Football

THE CASE OF THE BASKETBALL VIDEO

T.J. EDWARDS

ILLUSTRATED BY CHARLES TANG

A
LITTLE **APPLE**
PAPERBACK

SCHOLASTIC INC.
New York   Toronto   London   Auckland   Sydney

No part of this publication may be reproduced in whole or in part, or stored in a retrieval system, or transmitted in any form or by any means, electronic, mechanical, photocopying, recording, or otherwise, without written permission of the publisher. For information regarding permission, write to Scholastic Inc., 555 Broadway, New York, NY 10012.

ISBN 0-590-48455-9

Produced by Daniel Weiss Associates, Inc.
33 West 17th Street, New York, NY 10011

12 11 10 9 8 7 6 5 4 3 2 1   5 6 7 8 9/9 0/0

Printed in the U.S.A.   40

First Scholastic printing, December 1995

To Matt, Irwin, and Jonathan

THE CASE OF THE BASKETBALL VIDEO

A MYSTERIOUS INJURY

Bryan O'Malley aimed his video camera at the Ridgefield Community Center basketball court. The Smashers were playing the Ziffs in a close semifinal match.

"We destroyed the Hornets this morning," Bryan's friend Sam Jansen said from beside him. "It wasn't even close!"

Bryan didn't take his eye away from his camera. Through the viewfinder, he watched as the Smashers worked the ball up the court.

"How'd you like the way Jack drove to the hoop to draw a foul in the final seconds?" Sam asked. "He's a regular Penny Hardaway out there on the court."

Bryan sighed and looked up from his camera. "It was a great game," he said. "And Jack was amazing at the end, but—"

"He was just like Walt Frazier in the 1969 Championship Series!" Sam exclaimed. He was an expert in sports history. Bryan thought that Sam knew almost *too* much trivia—about every player on every team in every sport. "That's when the Lakers lost to the Knicks in seven games," Sam continued.

"Listen," Bryan told Sam. "Can we talk about the Knicks some other time? I've got to get this game on tape."

"I don't see why," Sam replied. "We're Smithfield Sonics—the best team in the league. We don't need to study a video."

"Don't forget that the Ziffs took us to overtime last month," Bryan said. "And the Smashers have Charlie Watts. He's a tough player. This video may help us figure out ways to keep his score down."

"Okay," Sam agreed with a sigh.

"Besides," Bryan continued, focusing the camera back on the court, "I've got to get some good footage for this year's contest."

"Contest?" Sam asked.

"The Ridgefield County junior filmmaker prize," Bryan said. "Remember? I came in first last year."

"I remember," Sam said, grinning. "All you got was a lousy plaque."

Bryan looked up from the camera. "So what?" he countered, running his hand through his red hair. "I still won. And this year the winner gets to spend an entire week at WBGA, the local news station. I'll get to learn all the insider stuff about how documentaries are really made."

"Well, that's an improvement," Sam said. "What's your film going to be about?"

"I've got a great topic," Bryan said

3

proudly. "Basketball in Ridgefield County. I'm also interviewing the players, the refs, the coaches—you know, getting the personal angle."

"It sounds interesting," Sam said. "Make sure you get a lot of close-ups of the best Sonic player—me!"

Bryan smiled and shook his head. Then he peered through the lens of his camera again. He felt confident about winning the prize this year. His only real competition would be Robin Mills, the girl who came in second last year.

But now he had to concentrate on what was happening on the court. It was five minutes into the third quarter and the Ziffs were up by ten points.

Bryan followed the action with his camera. The Ziffs' point guard, Peter Stacker, dribbled the ball upcourt, then bounced a pass to Ray Washington, the center, in the low post. With his back to the basket, Ray dribbled twice, faked left, and spun right. Then he sunk a fadeaway jumper.

Swish!

"Nothing but net!" Sam cried.

Bryan looked up from his camera. "See?" he said. "We're going to have to be careful tomorrow. Ray's a good four inches taller than me."

Ray, the Ziff star player, was one of the tallest eleven-year-olds in Ridgefield County. When he had the ball in his hands he was virtually unstoppable.

"We can't let the ball anywhere near him," Sam agreed. "And it'll be your job to force him away from the basket."

"It'll be pretty hard to keep him from going where he wants," Bryan said. "He's stronger than Shaquille O'Neal."

"Aw, you could take on Shaq," Sam teased with a smile.

"You're crazy," Bryan said and once again returned to his camera.

Charlie Watts, the Smashers' point guard and best player, was bringing the ball upcourt. Bryan watched him dribble right then left, while observing the court. He passed to the off-guard, then took a pass back and shot.

"Two points," Sam said.

"Charlie's got a sweet stroke," Bryan added.

Sam sighed. "I guess we've got our work cut out for us no matter who we play."

"We do," Bryan agreed, turning back to his camera. "And with their lead, it looks like it's going to be the Ziffs."

Just then Ray Washington powered his way into the lane and sunk a short fall-away jumper.

"He's unstoppable!" Sam exclaimed. "He reminds me of—"

Suddenly a shout from the court cut off Sam's words. Ray was on the floor clutching his ankle.

"What happened?" Sam asked.

"I don't know," Bryan replied. "I couldn't see clearly. Ray was just standing there and then a second later he was on the floor."

Bryan stopped his camera while the referee called for the Ziffs' coach. A man in a brown warm-up jacket hustled onto the floor and looked over Ray's ankle. The two teams gathered around and the fans stood quietly. After a few minutes, Bryan saw the referee and the coach help Ray to his feet and off the court.

"He's hobbling pretty bad," Bryan said. "Maybe I'll get a shot of it. You know, the agony of defeat and all that."

Bryan looked through his camera and focused on Ray. But the moment he pressed the record button, a dark shape passed in front of the lens.

"Hey!" Bryan exclaimed, looking up.

Standing right in front of him was Robin Mills, the girl he had beaten in last year's film contest. She had two pink baby doll clips in her blond hair.

"Robin, what do you think you're doing?" Bryan asked. "Trying to sabotage me? That's not going to win you any prizes, you know."

"Relax, it was an accident," Robin replied. "I needed to get by and tried to duck under your shot."

"Sure you did!" Bryan cried. "You tried to wreck my shot. I should—"

Bryan felt Sam's hand on his shoulder. "She said it was an accident," Sam said. "Calm down."

Bryan shook himself, suddenly embarrassed. "Yeah . . . I guess it's possible you were trying to duck out of the way."

"I was," Robin said, and she smiled.

Bryan held out his hand. "No hard feelings, okay?"

"No hard feelings," Robin agreed, shaking his hand.

"So what's your subject this year?" Sam asked.

Robin shook her head and pointed at Bryan. "If you think I'm going to tell you that in front of my main competition, you're crazy."

"I wouldn't steal your ideas," Bryan protested.

"Maybe not," Robin said. "But it's going to be a surprise."

"Why?" Bryan asked. "Doing another

8

film about a Halloween party?"

"No, dummy," Robin said. "That was last year. This year I've got a really great idea that's definitely going to get me into the WBGA TV station."

Bryan grinned. "If you think you can beat me, more power to you," he told Robin. "But I've got a film that'll knock those two hair clips straight off your head."

Robin put her hands on her hips. "We'll see about that," she said. Then she turned and walked out of the gym.

"She means business," Sam said. "I wonder what her film's going to be about?"

"Who knows?" Bryan replied. "Maybe a documentary on what it's like to come in second place behind a redheaded genius."

He turned back to his camera. Ray Washington was out for the rest of the game. And without Ray's large body to block the lane, Charlie Watts kept driving to the basket easily. If another Ziff player came over to cover him, Charlie passed to an open man for an uncontested shot. By the middle of the fourth quarter the Smashers were up by eight.

"It looks like we're going to be trying to stop Charlie tomorrow," Sam said, "and not the Ziffs."

"Looks that way," Bryan agreed. He glanced up from his camera and shook his head. "Too bad about Ray, though. I still don't know why he fell."

"This is basketball," Sam replied. "People fall and get hurt all the time. In the fifth game of the 1969 Championships—"

"Enough about 1969, already," Bryan joked. "Man, you know more sports trivia than anyone I've ever met. It's crazy!"

"No crazier than you and that video camera," Sam shot back. "Movies are all you ever think about."

Bryan smiled. "Okay, you've got me there. You're a sports nut and I'm a film nut."

"But first and foremost," Sam

declared with a wide grin, "we're the Smithfield Sonics!"

"And tomorrow we're going to smash the Smashers!" Bryan replied enthusiastically. "With me at center, you at power forward, Corey at small forward, and Jack and Lara at the guard positions—we can't miss."

"Speaking of Corey, Jack, and Lara," Sam said, "let's go show them this game film. Maybe we can figure out a defense against Charlie's killer drives to the hoop."

Just then the buzzer sounded. Bryan looked at the scoreboard where the final totals flashed in red: Smashers 68, Ziffs 59. "Smashers it is," he said, folding up his tripod. He tossed Sam his camera bag. "Carry this, okay?"

"You got it," Sam replied. "Now let's find the rest of the gang."

2

A CLUE IN SLO-MO

An hour later, Bryan and Sam were sitting with Lara Martini and Jack Cummings in the living room of Corey Johnstone's house, going over their strategy for the game against the Smashers. Jack announced to his teammates, "I can guard Charlie, no sweat."

"Are you sure?" Bryan asked. "Charlie's one fast guy off the tip-off."

"He's got great moves," Sam agreed.

Jack smiled. "So do I," he said.

"And Charlie's a little taller than you," Bryan added.

Jack's eyes narrowed. "So what if I'm a little on the short side. I can still run circles around Charlie Watts!"

"Relax," Lara Martini said. "We all know you're one of the best dribblers in the league."

"Right," Jack said. He looked at Sam and Bryan and grinned. "And don't you forget it."

"How can we?" Bryan replied. "You constantly remind us."

The door from the kitchen swung open. Corey pushed into the living room holding a tray of sandwiches.

"Lunchtime," she called. "We've got peanut butter and jelly, and ham and cheese."

"All right," Sam said. "Ham and cheese for me!"

"Why don't we eat while we watch the video?" Lara asked.

While Sam and Jack sat on the floor in front of the TV, Bryan put his video in the VCR.

"Get ready to witness filmmaking genius," Bryan bragged.

"Just press play," Jack sighed.

"Did Ray Washington really sprain his ankle?" Corey asked, reaching for a sandwich.

"He did," Sam replied, taking a seat on the couch. "But I'm not sure how. One second he was dominating both ends of the court and the next minute he was on the floor in pain."

"It was weird," Bryan said.

For the next fifteen minutes Jack and the gang ate and watched the game. Since the Smashers were going to be their opponent the next day, they didn't waste time analyzing Ray Washington's moves. The Sonics only paid serious attention to Charlie's drives to the hoop.

"He has a quick first step," Lara said, as Charlie breezed by a defender on the screen.

"He does," Jack admitted, "but I think I'm quick enough to keep up with him."

"Or we can all take turns guarding him," Sam suggested.

"That could work," Bryan said. "The more we tire Charlie out, the better we should do."

"But we've got to realize that Charlie is going to get his points," Corey said. "We can't let the rest of the Smashers sneak by us."

"That shouldn't be too difficult," Bryan said. "No one else is very good. We have a much more balanced offense."

"If Charlie does beat Jack and drive into the lane, we've got to foul him or make him pass to another teammate," Lara continued.

"Right," Jack said with a nod. "No easy baskets."

The five friends focused their attention back on the TV. Jack leaned closer to the set. Ray Washington flipped a ball through the hoop and then began jogging down-court, into a crowd of players. The next thing Jack knew, Ray was sprawled on the court clutching his ankle.

"Wow," Corey said. "It happened so fast."

15

"He must have stepped on it wrong," Sam added. "It was a freak accident."

But Jack wasn't so sure. A blur on the screen had caught his eye. It had been almost too quick to notice, but he knew he had seen *something*.

"Hey, Bryan," he said. "Could you play that again?"

Bryan wrinkled his brow. "Why?" he asked.

"Just play it," Jack insisted.

Bryan shrugged and pressed rewind on the remote control.

Jack moved closer to the screen. He watched Ray Washington jog back down the court. Once again, Ray cut through a crowd of people—and then suddenly hit the floor.

"Satisfied?" Sam asked.

"Not yet," Jack replied. "Can you play it in slow motion?"

Lara squinted at the television. "What do you see, Jack?" she asked.

"I think Ray might have been tripped," Jack replied.

The other four Sonics exchanged glances.

"On purpose?" Corey asked.

"I don't know yet," Jack said. "I've got to see it again."

Bryan rewound the tape and pressed play. This time the whole gang paid close attention. Once again, Ray Washington jogged lightly up the court.

"All right," Jack said. "Go to slo-mo right here."

Bryan pressed a button on the remote and the action on the screen slowed down.

"Even slower," Jack asked.

"Okay," Bryan answered. "But this is super slow. If you want it any slower you'll have to look at the video frame by frame."

On-screen, Ray inched into the crowd of players. Next to him were two other Ziffs and Charlie Watts. Then Jack saw Charlie's leg shoot out and sweep Ray off his feet.

"See?" Jack asked excitedly.

"Charlie Watts did that?" Corey asked. "I can't believe it."

"There's no way it was on purpose," Lara said. "Charlie's too nice. He's probably the best guy on my whole block."

"It had to be a mistake," Corey agreed.

"It didn't look like a mistake to me," Sam said. "Show it again, Bryan."

Seconds later, the gang once again saw Charlie sweep Ray's feet out from under him.

Lara sighed heavily. "We don't have much choice. I guess we have to investigate."

"Man, Lara," Sam said, "you're always thinking like a detective."

The rest of the gang smiled. Lara, one of the brightest students at Jefferson Elementary School, read at least two mystery novels a week.

"Well, we *are* detectives," Lara reminded the gang. "We've solved three cases already."

"That's true," Corey said.

"And maybe now we've got a fourth.

Charlie lives on my block," Lara said. "We should pay him a visit, and hear his side of the story."

"Okay," Bryan said. "But not until I finish my PB and J."

A half hour later the gang stood on Charlie Watts's doorstep.

"Did you remember the tape?" Jack asked.

"Sure did," Bryan replied.

Jack nodded and rang the bell. After a moment, a dark-haired girl with glasses opened the door. It was Marianne, Charlie's younger sister.

"Hi," Marianne said. "You're the Sonics, right? What brings you guys over here?"

"We need to ask Charlie a few questions," Jack said.

Marianne wrinkled her brow. "Questions? About what?"

"Nothing serious," Lara said. "Just something we think we might have seen on a videotape."

Marianne nodded. "Sounds mysterious. You'd better come in."

Marianne swung the door open and ushered the Sonics into her family's living room. "I think Charlie's watching a video," she said. She looked down a stairway and called, "Hey, Charlie!"

There was no response.

"Charlie!" Marianne called again.

This time Jack heard a muffled answer. "What?"

"You've got company!"

"What?" Charlie asked again loudly from downstairs.

"Company!" Marianne yelled.

"Okay, okay!" Charlie replied. "I'm coming!"

"That's just like me when I'm watching a video," Bryan said. "I forget the rest of the world even exists."

"He'll be right up," Marianne said. "I'll get you guys something to drink while you're waiting." She turned and went to the kitchen.

After Marianne had left, Lara said,

"See? The whole family is so nice."

Charlie suddenly clattered up the stairs. When he saw the Sonics, he grinned broadly. "Have you come to forfeit the game before we even step on the court?" he asked jokingly.

Lara smiled. "You wish," she said.

"It was worth a try," Charlie replied.

"What video were you watching?" Bryan asked.

"*Lethal Planet, Part Three*," Charlie answered.

Jack saw Bryan's eyes nearly pop out of his head. "My favorite!" Bryan cried.

"One of mine, too," Charlie said.

"It's pretty hard to find, though," Bryan said. "The only store in Smithfield that has it is BigTime Video."

"That's where I rent all my films," Charlie replied. "They've got the best selection. Last week I saw *Revenge of the Purple Body Snatchers*."

"That's a great movie," Bryan said solemnly. "It's got an excellent shot of mummified heads in the—"

"I'm sure the mummified heads are just great," Jack cut in, "but we've come to ask you a quick question, Charlie."

"A question?" Charlie asked. "Shoot."

The gang exchanged awkward glances, and even Jack felt nervous about accusing Charlie. "Well—" Jack began.

"I mixed up some lemonade," Marianne interrupted, coming out of the kitchen. She held a big tray of drinks in her hands.

After Jack had accepted a glass of lemonade, he tried to continue. "You see, Charlie. It's like this. Bryan was taping today's game—"

"For a documentary I'm doing," Bryan added. He rummaged through his bag and then held up the videotape.

"And we were looking at the film a little while ago—" Corey put in.

"When we saw something sort of funny," Sam finished.

"We're sure it's nothing, of course,"

Lara said. "But we had to ask."

"Then ask," Charlie said. "Man, you guys are acting weird! What's going on?"

Again, the gang exchanged awkward glances.

"You say it, Jack," Bryan said finally. "You were the one who noticed it."

Jack sighed. Then he turned to Charlie. "We watched the tape and saw you trip Ray Washington," he blurted out.

For a moment no one spoke. Jack saw Charlie's face turn red. He didn't know if Charlie was going to hit him or cry, but then he nodded once and sat on the sofa.

"I did trip Ray," he admitted softly.

Jack heard Lara gasp. "You did?" she asked.

"Yes," Charlie explained. "But by accident!" He looked mournfully at the gang. "We were all bunched up and my legs got tangled with his. Next thing I knew he was on the ground and out of the game. I feel terrible."

For a moment no one spoke. Charlie buried his head in his hands.

"It's okay, Charlie," Lara said after a moment. "We believe you."

"I was going to tell the ref," Charlie said, "but the whole thing happened so fast. Then I got scared that I'd get in trouble."

"I probably would've felt that way, too," Sam said.

"Maybe I should write a note to Ray," Charlie suggested. "You know, apologize to him."

"That's probably not necessary," Jack said. "These things happen in sports all the time."

"Right," Sam said excitedly. "Like to Willis Reed in the 1969 NBA Finals!"

Bryan covered his eyes with his hands. "Sam, please don't start on the trivia again," he said.

"We're sorry to have bothered you," Lara told Charlie. "Get back to that movie and we'll see you tomorrow on the court."

Charlie stood up. "Right. Tomorrow.

And I promise—no more accidents!"

"And may the best team win," Jack added. "The *Sonics!*"

Charlie flashed his friendly smile again. "We'll see about that, Jack. We'll see about that."

3

LARA CAN'T MISS

Early the next afternoon, the Sonics sat together on the bench at the community center, ready for their championship showdown against the Smashers. Game time was five minutes away and both teams had completed their layup drills. Lara watched the referee, a young man named Mr. Crimmins, as he paced the floor, dribbling a basketball. She looked over her shoulder. The stands were full with fans. Vendors sold hot dogs, sodas, and ice cream.

"There's a big turnout today," Lara whispered to Corey.

Corey glanced around. "There sure is. The pressure's on."

Lara heard a familiar voice pierce through the crowd. "Go get 'em, Sonics! Take that ball to the hoop, you hear? Easy transition baskets! That's what wins games!" Lara and Corey exchanged a smile as they spotted Mr. Hanraddy, the Jefferson Elementary School's registrar, in the crowd. He was the Sonics most loyal fan. No matter what sport the team played—baseball, soccer, football, or basketball—he was there cheering them on.

Lara waved to the old man, and then turned back to the bench. Bryan and Sam were practicing shooting imaginary free throws while Jack laced up his high-tops. The other three Sonics, Joe Tanksley, Peter Fisk, and Marla Armstrong, sat on the bench quietly, waiting for their time on the court.

Suddenly Mr. Lester, the Sonics'

coach, hurried toward the bench.

"All right, team," he said. "Let's huddle up, now. Big game! Big game!"

The Sonics gathered around their coach. Mr. Lester brushed a strand of hair off his bald spot and reached for his calculator. The gang smiled at each other. Mr. Lester, an accountant by profession, was known for his unusual pep talks.

"Let's see," Mr. Lester said, punching some figures into his calculator. "Please don't forget that the team that shoots the highest percentage of free throws often wins. So take the ball to the hoop. Don't be scared to draw a few fouls." The coach began to pace. "Play good team basketball, pass the ball, look for the open man, and I'm sure we'll do just fine." He stopped pacing and turned abruptly to face the team. "That reminds me," he said. "The other night I had an urge to reread some Pythagoras, the great Greek mathematician. He had a few things to say that relate to the game of hoops. For instance—"

A buzzer sounded, interrupting Mr. Lester's pep talk. He looked confused.

"Okay," the referee called over. "Let's get this show on the road."

"But I didn't get to finish," Mr. Lester complained. "Oh, well. Team, we've practiced hard over the past few weeks, and we've made it all the way to the finals. Now go out there and win!"

Lara stood up, her heart beating rapidly. *Pregame jitters,* she thought.

The Sonics put their hands together, shouted "Go!," and then took the court. The Smashers were already waiting. Jack and Charlie shook hands and Bryan lined up opposite the Smasher center, a lanky boy named John Willows. Lara shook hands with the opposite off-guard, Brenda Frazier.

"Good luck," Lara said to her opponent.

Brenda nodded.

"Okay, kids," the referee called. "Let's

have a good clean game. No cheap fouls."

Lara crouched into position. Bryan often tapped the ball to her. Concentrating hard, she saw the referee toss the ball in the air. Then Bryan jumped—but not high enough. John Willows tipped the ball straight to Charlie. Charlie grabbed the ball, took off downcourt like a shot, and put the ball in for an easy two points.

"Get back on defense!" Mr. Hanraddy cried.

Lara agreed with Mr. Hanraddy's advice. The Sonics had to play solid defense or else Charlie would beat them down the court every time.

"All right, team!" Mr. Lester called. "It's only two points. Let's get the next eighty!"

Jack dribbled the ball upcourt. Lara ran ahead of him and took the right wing while Bryan fought for position in the low post. Meanwhile, Sam spread wide to the left and Corey dashed across the court, trying to get open for a pass.

Jack kept dribbling. Charlie moved in close and tried to use his quick reflexes to flick the ball away. But Jack protected the ball and passed to Lara. Lara dribbled twice and passed back to Jack. He dribbled once, faked left, and then zipped by Charlie and sunk a basket.

"Nice move," Lara heard Charlie say to Jack.

"Thanks," Jack replied. He jogged down the court to play defense.

Charlie took the inbounds pass, pushed the ball downcourt, and drove to the hoop again. This time, instead of finishing the play by himself, he looped a pass behind his back to John Willows in the low post. The tall boy put up a weak hook shot. Lara saw Bryan box out the Smasher strong forward and reel in the rebound.

And Sam took off downcourt.

"Look!" Lara yelled. Bryan glanced where Lara was pointing, cocked his arm, and hurled the ball—a perfect pass. Sam caught it on the run, dribbled once, and laid it in for another two points.

"We've got to get back on defense!" Lara heard Charlie tell his team. "No easy baskets!"

The Smasher off-guard passed to Charlie, who ran the ball upcourt again. Jack stuck to him like glue and Charlie passed off to Hal Michaels, the Smashers' small forward. Hal bounced a pass to John Willows. This time the tall boy turned and shot over Bryan's outstretched hands for two more points.

"Charlie makes everything happen for them," Lara said to Sam as she jogged back upcourt.

"He sure does," Sam agreed.

Lara spread wide to the right with Sam. Jack dribbled the ball down the left side while Bryan struggled for position in the low post. "I'm open!" Bryan called, waving his arms.

Jack bounced a pass. Bryan dribbled

twice, pivoted on his left foot, then turned and shot.

"Nothing but net!" Lara heard Corey cry.

Once again, Charlie charged upcourt with the ball.

"Defense!" Lara cried. "Get tough!"

During the rest of the half, the Sonics played solid team basketball, passing the ball and finding the open man. They got back on defense and rebounded well. But somehow Charlie found a way to keep the Smashers' hopes alive. Each time he ran down the court, he drove to the hoop and set up teammates for big plays. In fact, midway through the second quarter, the Smashers were up by eight.

Then Lara got hot. With four minutes to go in the half and the Sonics' confidence fading, Lara felt a tingling in her fingers. She grabbed a pass from Jack, stepped behind the three-point line and took a shot.

Bulls'-eye!

After a Smasher turnover, Corey

brought the ball up the court. Lara positioned herself behind the three-point line again. Corey, who knew about Lara's hot streaks, fired the ball to her. Lara took aim and shot. *Swish!*

The crowd rose to its feet, cheering wildly.

"Nothing but net!" Mr. Hanraddy shouted.

On his next run down the court, Charlie sunk a three-pointer of his own. By the time the Sonics got the ball back to Lara, a Smasher was on her like glue. Lara faked a shot, and drove to the hoop. She passed off to Corey, who was free under the basket.

With a minute left in the half, the Sonics were down by two. Another basket by Lara at the buzzer tied the game at 44.

"Way to go, Lara!" Jack cried as the team headed for the locker room.

Corey slapped Lara on the back. "You got us back in the running," she told her friend.

"Thanks," Lara said. "But we've got to find some way to slow down Charlie."

"Right," Sam said.

"Let's hit the Coaches' locker room and see what Mr. Lester has to say," Lara suggested.

"I'll meet you guys there," Bryan called from the bench.

Lara looked up to see Bryan holding his camera and tripod.

"What're you doing?" she asked.

"I hear there's a good halftime show—a group of jugglers from Smithfield Junior High," Bryan replied. "I thought I'd catch it for my documentary."

"This isn't the time to be thinking about your film!" Jack scolded.

"Jack's right," Corey said. "We've got to go to the Coaches' locker room."

"I'll just point the camera at the court," Bryan said, setting up the tripod. "Then I'll put it on automatic and see what I get. It'll only take a second."

*   *   *

Lara stood with her teammates outside the Coaches' locker room, waiting for Mr. Lester. Moments later, the coach bustled down the hallway.

"First things first," he said. "I like a lot of what I'm seeing out there. You're really hustling, diving for those loose balls, boxing out for rebounds and looking for the open man. That's how this game should be played."

"But what about Charlie?" Bryan asked.

Mr. Lester pointed a finger at the ceiling. "I've got just the thing."

"What?" Sam asked.

Mr. Lester took out his calculator and began punching numbers on the pad. "According to my calculations, we should have someone larger guard Charlie."

Jack took a step toward the coach. "But—"

"Sorry," Mr. Lester interrupted. "You've been playing a fine game, Jack. But I want to try out Sam on Charlie for a while. Sam, cover Charlie all the way up the court. Tire him out."

"I got it," Sam said with a nod. "It's what Scottie Pippen did to Magic Johnson in the 1991 Championship Series."

"Right," Mr. Lester cut in. "Sam, don't let Charlie control the tempo of the game. Now let's go out there and pulverize the Smashers!"

After a short break, the Sonics returned to the court. As she took her warm-up shots, Lara still felt the tingling in her fingers, but knew she couldn't count on staying hot the entire game. She also knew that Mr. Lester's plan might backfire and Sam might not be able to keep up with speedy Charlie.

"All right!" the referee announced. "Let's keep things moving along."

Lara sunk a final practice shot, and then jogged to her bench.

"Hey!" she heard someone cry. "Watch it."

Lara shook her head. She had been thinking so hard about the game that she had nearly run into Robin Mills. "Sorry," she said.

"No problem," Robin replied. "I'm sorry I snapped at you, but I've got all this camera equipment."

Robin held up a brand new video camera. In her other hand was a hot dog.

"What're you doing here?" Lara asked. "Videotaping the game?"

"Nope," Robin replied. "I'm just working on the junior filmmaker competition."

"What's your film about?" Lara asked.

Robin smiled. "That's none of your business right now," she said.

Just then the buzzer rang. "Come on, Lara!" Mr. Lester cried. "Second half!"

"Well, I've got to run," Robin said. "Good luck in the rest of the game."

Lara watched Robin scurry across the court and disappear into the stands. Robin was acting normal enough, but Lara had a feeling she was up to something. *I wonder what it could be?* Lara thought.

"Come on, Lara!" Bryan called.

Lara turned back to the bench. She felt the tingle in her fingers. *First things first,* she thought. *We've got a game to win!*

No Accident

From the first moment Charlie touched the ball, Sam put Mr. Lester's plan into effect, constantly keeping the Smashers' star covered.

"New strategy, huh?" Charlie said to Sam with a grin as he pushed the ball upcourt.

"Right," Sam answered.

But Charlie didn't appear to be fazed, making up for Sam's defense with an extra dose of determination. It took him longer to get the ball upcourt, but he still ran the offense to perfection.

Luckily for the Sonics, Lara picked up right where she had left off at the end of the first half. Almost every shot she took went in.

"Man," Sam told her halfway through the third quarter, "you're like Reggie Miller in game five of the Indiana–New York series in 1994."

"Oh, really?" Lara replied.

"Enough chat," Sam heard Bryan yell. "We haven't won the game yet. Play defense!"

Sam sighed and hustled over to Charlie.

"Keep up that pressure!" Sam heard Mr. Hanraddy call from the first row. "Tire him out!"

"Hang in there, Sam!" Mr. Lester called.

But Sam soon felt winded, while Charlie barely seemed to break a sweat. With four minutes to go in the third quarter, Sam asked for a breather.

"Okay," Mr. Lester said to Joe Tanksley. "Your turn. Try to slow Charlie down. Constant pressure. Odds are he'll crack soon!"

Sam collapsed on the bench, took a long gulp of water, and turned his eyes to the court. Corey had the ball on the left. She passed to Jack at the top of the key. Sam could tell Jack wanted to shoot, but Charlie was right on him. Jack passed back to Corey who dribbled twice and lofted a pass across court to Lara. Lara faked a shot and whipped a low pass to Bryan.

"Put it in!" Sam called.

And Bryan did, tying the score at 58.

Sam glanced at the clock. Two minutes left in the quarter. Mr. Lester did some more substituting now, sending in Peter Fisk and Marla Armstrong for Jack and Corey.

"Good work out there," Sam said to his two buddies as they sat on the bench next to him.

"Thanks," Bryan said. "This is going to go to the wire, though. That's for sure."

"I just hope Lara stays hot!" Corey said.

Sam nodded and looked to the court. Lara drove to the hoop and nailed a ten-footer.

"No problems there," Sam said. "She's on fire."

The quarter ended with the Sonics up by three.

"OK," Mr. Lester said, gathering the team around. "Remember what they say in the NBA, team. During the playoffs, defense wins. So get tough. Contest every shot. Box out for those rebounds. Dive for every loose ball!"

The team nodded. As the buzzer sounded, Sam took another long drink of water.

"Okay," Mr. Lester said. "Starting lineup back on the court. Sam, you stay on Charlie."

Sam nodded and jogged to the court. He knew he had been given the dirty work. His job wasn't to score points but to do whatever he could to stop the other

team's star. It wasn't glamorous but it was vitally important. Unfortunately, Sam couldn't do a thing to slow down the Smasher star. The next time he moved down the court, Charlie hit a three-pointer.

There's no stopping that guy! Sam thought.

Luckily for the Sonics, there was no stopping Lara, either. The final quarter of the game became a one-on-one contest. Nearly every time Lara got her hands on the ball, she scored. But each shot was answered by another from Charlie.

After Lara sank a perfect layup, Charlie ran behind her and stuck out his foot. In a flash—almost too fast for Sam to see—Lara fell to the floor, clutching her ankle. Play stopped instantly. The referee, both teams, and both coaches gathered around her.

"What's the problem?" Mr. Lester asked. Lara was on the floor, holding her foot.

"It's my bad ankle," she moaned.

The gang exchanged woeful glances. Earlier that year, Lara had missed a key football game due to a sprained ankle.

Mr. Lester pressed Lara's right ankle lightly. "Does it hurt here?" he asked.

Lara winced. "Yes, yes. It hurts!"

Mr. Lester nodded. "You're through for the day."

Sam frowned. He watched with growing anger as Mr. Lester helped Lara to her feet and off the court. The rest of the Sonics were upset, but Sam was furious.

"Charlie did it!" he hissed to Bryan.

"Are you sure?" Bryan asked.

Before Sam could reply, Charlie walked up to Bryan.

"It's such a shame," Charlie said. "We had such a good competition going."

"Oh, like you really care!" Sam snapped.

Charlie blinked. "What's the matter, Sam?"

"You tripped her!" Sam exclaimed, his face red. "I saw you."

Charlie's eyes went wide. "Tripped her? No way! I'd never do something like that. You're seeing things."

"Is there some sort of problem here?" the referee asked.

"Only that Charlie is a cheater!" Sam cried.

Suddenly, everyone was talking at once. With each denial Charlie made, Sam became angrier and angrier.

"I saw it!" Sam exclaimed. "He stuck out his foot!"

The next thing Sam knew, Mr. Lester was holding him firmly by the shoulders.

"I don't like this one bit," the referee said. "Perhaps you think you saw something, but I can't imagine that Charlie would trip another player. I've known Charlie a long time, and he's always played by the rules."

"But I saw it!" Sam protested. "He did it yester—"

"Enough! Hit the bench, son!" the referee barked.

Sam blinked. "The bench?"

"You heard me," the referee snapped. "And I'll expect a letter of apology if you ever care to play in this league again!"

"Come on, Sam," Mr. Lester said gently.

"But—" Sam began.

"Off the court!" the referee ordered.

Sam had never felt angrier. Fuming, he broke away from Mr. Lester and collapsed on the end of the bench.

"Hang in there!" Mr. Lester called to the team. "Tough defense!"

But Sam knew that was impossible. Without Lara's hot hand to balance out Charlie, the Sonics were doomed. Bryan tried an inside move but his shot was stuffed by John Willows. Corey drove to the basket and was called for charging. Jack went to the free-throw line but missed both shots. By the time the final buzzer sounded, the Sonics had lost by twelve.

No one was more frustrated than Sam. Not only had he spent the entire first half being embarrassed by the speedier Charlie, he had also witnessed a crime.

"We were robbed!" he told the gang on the sidelines as the Smashers celebrated at midcourt. "Charlie tripped Lara. I swear it! We've got another case!"

"That sneak!" Jack said. "I'd like to show him a thing or two."

"Relax," Corey said. "We need proof."

"We've got proof!" Sam cried. "I saw it!"

"He'll deny it, though," Bryan said. "It's just your word against his."

"He *already* denied it," Sam said. "And the ref believed him!"

"Why don't we ask Lara?" Corey suggested. "She'll probably know what happened."

Moments later, the gang was in the Coaches' tiny locker room. Lara was sitting on a bench, with her ankle wrapped in ice.

"It all happened so fast," she said. "One second I was moving toward the basket, and the next second I was down. I guess someone might have tripped me, but I couldn't say who."

"So you didn't see Charlie do it?" Jack asked.

"No," Lara answered. "I was looking the other way."

"Well, I know what I saw!" Sam insisted.

"Relax," Bryan said. "We believe you. If only we had some more proof—"

"Wait a second," Jack interrupted, his eyes lighting up. "We do!"

"What?" Lara asked.

"Bryan's camera!" Jack answered.

"That's right!" Bryan said excitedly. "I never turned it off and it was pointed straight at the court."

Without a further word, the Sonics rushed back into the gym. Lara hobbled along with them on her crutches as fast as she could.

"Well?" Jack asked as Bryan inspected the camera.

"I can't believe it!" Bryan exclaimed.

"You can't believe what?" Sam asked.

Bryan looked and met Sam's eyes. "Someone turned it off!"

"Are you sure?" Corey asked.

"Yes, I'm sure," Bryan said. "Unless it clicked off magically. It was only on for five minutes. I didn't even get all of the half-time show!"

"But who would've turned off your camera?" Corey asked.

"Who else?" Bryan said. "Robin! She's trying to sabotage my documentary."

"But when?" Sam asked.

"When we were in the Coaches' locker room during the break," Jack replied. "She had plenty of time."

"And I saw her around here just after halftime," Lara said.

"Hey," Sam said suddenly. "What's this?" He pointed to a small puddle in front of the camera.

"Don't ask me," Lara said. "But it's not raining inside this building, so someone must have spilled it." She turned to Bryan. "Did you spill anything when you were setting up the camera?"

"Nope," Bryan said.

"Maybe it'll help us prove Robin turned off the camera," Sam said. "It's evidence."

"Okay, it's evidence," Lara agreed. "But what is it?"

"I have no idea," Sam said. "Why don't you taste it and see?"

"Taste it?" Lara cried. "Off of the floor?"

"Why not?" Sam asked. "It's our only evidence. We've got to know what it is."

"Then *you* taste it!" Lara said. "I'm not going to—"

"Oh, I'll do it," Jack interrupted. He dropped to his knees and sniffed at the puddle.

"What do you smell?" Corey asked, kneeling next to him.

"Your sneakers," Jack replied. "Could you take a few steps back?"

"Oops, sorry," Corey said, and she moved away from Jack.

Jack continued to sniff. After a few seconds, he rose to his feet, his eyes gleaming.

"Grape drink!" he announced.

"Grape drink?" Sam asked. "You can tell that quickly?"

Jack nodded. "My nose doesn't lie. I practically live on the stuff during the summer. You want to sniff?"

"That's okay," Bryan said. "We'll take your word for it."

"All right," Lara said. "I did see Robin eating a hot dog . . . she could have had something to drink, too. Maybe we should try and find out whether Robin likes grape drink."

"We should," Sam said. "But the fact remains that Charlie tripped you. I saw it. He's a cheater. I don't care how nice a guy he is. I say we turn him in, using Bryan's tape from yesterday showing him tripping Ray Washington."

The gang was silent for a moment.

"But he's such a good—" Corey began.

"That doesn't matter," Sam broke in. "He's a cheater. Not only that, he hurt Lara!"

Corey sighed. "You're right."

"So we're agreed, then?" Lara said.

One by one, Sam saw his friends nod.

"Good," Sam said. "Let's get Bryan's tape of the Smasher–Ziff game and find the ref."

THE SWITCH

A half hour later the gang stood in front of a large red brick house around the corner from both Lara's and Corey's houses.

"Well, here we are," Corey said.

"You sure this is where the ref lives?" Sam asked.

"Positive," Corey said. "I see him mowing the lawn every Sunday afternoon." She rang the bell.

A few moments later the door swung open. Standing in the doorway in gray slacks and a blue cardigan sweater was

Mr. Crimmins, the referee. In his right hand was a pipe.

"Well, if it isn't the Smithfield Sonics." He smiled at Sam. "Come to fire me for benching you today? It's pretty bad form to accuse the opposing star of cheating, you know."

"I know, but I wasn't—" Sam began to protest.

"Relax, Sam," Bryan interrupted. He turned to the referee. "We think you did a pretty good job out there today."

Corey saw Mr. Crimmins's eyes open wide, surprised. "I'm shocked. You really think I called a good game, huh?"

"Sure you did," Lara said, leaning forward on her crutches.

"Except you should've called three seconds a few times against John Willows," Jack said. "I mean that guy practically lived in the paint."

Mr. Crimmins laughed. "Now that's what a ref expects to hear. Why don't you kids come in for some lemonade."

"We'd love to," Corey said.

Moments later, the gang was settled in Mr. Crimmins's living room. The referee leaned back in a red easy chair and took a deep puff from his pipe.

"I've called some close games in my time, kids," he said with a faraway look in his eyes. "And a ref's job isn't easy, you know. So many things to watch for: traveling, hand-checking, illegal defenses."

"Three seconds," Jack whispered to Corey.

Corey saw Mr. Crimmins wrinkle his brow. "What was that, son?"

"No . . . nothing—" Jack said quickly. "I said 'great lemonade.'"

To prove his point, Jack drank his entire glass in a gulp.

The referee nodded. "Nothing like a cool drink of lemonade. No, sir. The life of a referee isn't all it's cracked up to be. It takes work." The man leaned forward in his chair. "Did you children know that I practice throwing the ball up for tip-offs every morning?"

"Wow," Lara said. "That sure is interesting. But actually, sir, we had another reason—"

"It's not as easy as it looks to run up and down the court with a whistle in your mouth, either," Mr. Crimmins continued.

"I'm sure that's very difficult, sir," Bryan said. "But, you see, we dropped by to show you something."

Mr. Crimmins raised his eyebrows. "Show me something?"

Bryan reached into his film bag and pulled out the tape.

"A video?" Mr. Crimmins asked. "What is it? A referee guide?"

"No, no," Corey said. "Nothing like that. It's actually a video of yesterday's Smasher–Ziff game."

Mr. Crimmins sat up in his chair. "The Smashers and the Ziffs?"

"Right," Bryan said. "You see, I was filming the game as part of a documentary film project, and well . . ."

It took the Sonics a while, but they finally explained the reason for their visit. By the time they were through, Mr. Crimmins was pacing the floor, puffing furiously on his pipe.

"Charlie Watts a cheater?" he said. "I still can't believe it. But you say you have proof, eh?"

"Right on the tape, sir," Corey said.

Mr. Crimmins sighed. "I do hope you children are wrong," he said. "But if you're right, I'll be the first to apologize to you, Sam. But it is hard to believe. Charlie seems like such a fine boy. Well, I suppose I should take a look. Let's slip it in the old VCR."

Corey nodded to Bryan who handed the video to Mr. Crimmins. The gang anxiously gathered around the referee's large color TV. Mr. Crimmins sat back in his easy chair, pressed a button on the remote, and settled in to watch.

"The opening shot is of the outside of the community center," Bryan said. "You see, I'm doing a film on basketball in Smithfield, but covering it from the personal side, interviewing the coaches and players. Even the vendors. You would be surprised at . . ."

Bryan continued to talk, but Corey wasn't listening. The video had started but there was no community center. In fact, there was nothing on the screen that even closely resembled anything in the town of Smithfield.

"Oh, no!" Lara cried.

Corey blinked. It was hard to believe, but there on the screen was a picture of what appeared to be a herd of giant elk. An announcer said, "Welcome to *National Nature Weekly*. This week we look at the migration habits of the caribou."

Corey looked to Bryan, her heart beating fast. "Is this the right tape?"

"I sure thought so," Bryan said.

"It sure doesn't look like basketball to me," Mr. Crimmins said. "Now I may not be able to see every three-second violation, but I sure know a herd of caribou isn't a basketball team!"

The gang exchanged awkward glances. Corey saw Bryan desperately rummaging through his film bag.

"It's not there?" she asked.

Bryan shook his head. "Someone must have switched the tape."

"Could you have left it somewhere else?" Sam asked.

"No way," Bryan said. "It was in my film bag all the time."

"Maybe this is the right one," Mr. Crimmins suggested, "but you forgot about this little segment at the beginning."

"It *looks* like the right tape," Bryan said. "But I doubt I forgot what's in my own documentary!"

"Fast forward and see," Lara said.

Mr. Crimmins pressed another button on the remote. Suddenly, the gang was watching herds of caribou migrating very quickly. After a few moments it became clear that this tape didn't contain even a single frame of basketball action.

"Well, kids," Mr. Crimmins said. "It's not that I don't believe you." Corey saw the man look right at her. "I've known you for years and know you wouldn't come here unless you thought you were on to something. But accusing a boy like Charlie Watts is serious business. And as I said on the court today, it's awfully hard to believe. You'd better find that tape. Until you do, I'm going to forget this whole visit ever happened, okay?"

"Okay, Mr. Crimmins," Corey said, greatly embarrassed. "I guess we should be going."

The referee nodded. "Right. And if you find that missing tape, you know where to find me."

Bryan took the "Caribou" tape from the VCR. After some embarrassed good-byes, the gang found themselves on Mr. Crimmins's front doorstep.

"Are you sure you didn't switch the tapes yourself, by accident?" Jack asked.

"Sure, I'm sure!" Bryan said. "I've never watched a video on caribou in my life. I barely know what they are."

"They're related to elk and moose," Sam said. "And live in Alaska."

"Gee, thanks," Bryan said. "I feel so educated right now and . . . hey! Wait a minute!"

"What is it?" Lara asked.

"It *was* switched!" Bryan exclaimed. "I've got proof! Look, here," he said, pointing at the side of the video. "The label is almost the same as my tape, with this blue stripe. But look here: In tiny letters in the corner, it says 'BTV.' I never use that brand. Someone took the tape of the Smasher–Ziff game and replaced it with this."

"But who?" Lara asked.

"How about our prime suspect?" Corey suggested. "Robin."

"Don't overlook Charlie," Sam added. "He could've wanted to hide the evidence."

"Or maybe it was another Smasher," Bryan put in. "Charlie is their star and anyone on that team might want to cover for him."

"True," Lara said. "And don't forget Charlie's sister."

"Marianne?" Corey asked. "She was nice."

"So was Charlie," Jack observed.

"Okay," Lara said. "So we've got a good list of suspects. Now when was the tape switched?"

"It had to be during halftime," Bryan said. "I've had my film bag with me every other second. During the half, I left it by our bench."

Lara leaned forward on her crutches, her eyes wide. "Don't forget that I saw Robin walking away from the bench just before the third quarter."

"I knew I couldn't trust her!" Bryan exclaimed. "She's the one."

"We don't know that for sure," Lara said. "But maybe a look at the crime scene will tell us something."

With Lara hobbling, it took the gang a half hour to walk back to the community center. The building was closed, but Bryan, who had filmed the entire custodial staff for his documentary, got Mr. LeBlanc, the janitor, to let them in.

"Don't be long, you hear?" the janitor said in his French accent.

"Don't worry," Bryan replied. "And thanks. You'll get a big credit in my film for this."

Mr. LeBlanc whistled. *"Mon Dieu!"* he exclaimed. "I am the big movie star."

"Come on," Jack said, impatiently. "Let's get to the bench."

The gang hustled across the basketball floor to the bench their team had used. Corey looked around the big empty gym. With no cheering fans or practicing teams in it, the community center seemed eerie. She shuddered and looked at Jack, who was already on his hands and knees, searching under the bench.

"Find anything?" Lara called, hobbling behind.

"Nothing yet," Jack answered. "Hey, could we get a little more light in here?"

Corey saw Bryan look at Mr. LeBlanc. "I'll see what I can do," the janitor said.

The gang waited patiently. After a moment the gym was flooded with its usual amount of light.

"This is light enough for you?" the janitor called.

"Perfect!" Bryan yelled back.

Jack kept searching on his hands and knees. Suddenly, something glinted off the bright lights and caught Corey's eye.

"Hey, everyone," she said, pointing. "Look!"

"What is it?" Sam asked.

"I'm not sure yet," Corey replied. She dropped to her knees and picked up a small piece of orange metal from under the bench.

"It's a baby doll hair clip," Lara said.

Corey saw Sam and Bryan exchange a glance. "Robin wears hair clips like that," Sam said.

"Looks like we've got our crook," Jack said. "And I'll bet she loves grape drink, too."

"It's possible," Lara said. "But we should still look for witnesses. Maybe someone saw someone else hanging around our bench during halftime. And we should talk to Robin."

"I'm with you," Corey said. "And the sooner the better. We've got to get that stolen tape back."

"Right," Sam said. "I want to prove Charlie's a cheater and then I want a rematch. Then we'll smash the Smashers to bits."

6

A Clue in the Middle of Caribou

"I know who we should ask next," Jack said.

"Who?" Lara asked.

"The scorekeeper," he replied.

"Good idea," Bryan said with a nod. "He was here during halftime."

"And Mr. Hanraddy!" Sam said. "Don't forget him. He sits right behind our bench."

"Perfect," Jack said. "Now we're getting somewhere. Let's go over to the school. I'll bet Mr. Hanraddy is there right now. He catches up on paperwork on Sunday afternoons."

The community center wasn't very far away from Jefferson Elementary, where all the Sonics went to school. After a short walk, the gang knocked on Mr. Hanraddy's window.

The old man peeked through the glass and smiled. "Well, well," he said. "If it isn't the basketball stars. Come around front and I'll let you in."

Moments later, the gang was in Mr. Hanraddy's office. Sam grinned widely. The old man had posters and mementos dating back to the 1950s. For a sports trivia fanatic like Sam, Mr. Hanraddy's office was a treasure chest.

"I'm the oldest Sonics' fan around," Mr. Hanraddy said with a nod toward his walls. "Look there. That's the Smithfield Sonics in 1959. Fielded a fine team that year. Of course, they didn't let girls play back then. Times have certainly changed for the better." He winked at Lara. "Those fellows in the fifties could've used a shooter like you."

Lara blushed. "Thanks, Mr. Hanraddy."

The old man lowered himself into his chair. His desk was cluttered with papers and an old manual typewriter. "So, kids . . . to what do I owe the pleasure of this little visit?"

"Well," Jack began. "It's like this . . ."

Mr. Hanraddy listened to the Sonics' story carefully, every so often scratching the gray stubble on his chin.

"I wish I could help you," he said when Jack was through, "but I wasn't in the stands during halftime either."

"You weren't?" Sam asked. "I thought that—"

"You thought wrong, my friend," Mr. Hanraddy interrupted. "I had a hankering for something sweet so I went to the concession stand. Being old makes me sort of slow. By the time I got there that darned line was so long it took the whole halftime to get a small bag of caramel popcorn. So I didn't see a thing."

After they said good-bye to Mr. Hanraddy, the gang walked out to the school parking lot.

"Let's not give up yet," Jack said. "It's time to find the scorekeeper."

"Jake O'Connell is his name, I think," Sam said.

"Where does he live?" Jack asked.

"Who knows?" Corey said. "Let's go to my place and find a phone book."

After another short walk, the Sonics settled into Corey's kitchen. Jack began flipping through the white pages.

"Aha!" he cried. "O'Connell." Jack picked up the phone and dialed. "I'll handle this," he told his friends.

"I'll put him on the speaker phone," Corey said.

"Wow," Sam said. "Pretty modern."

The Sonics could hear the phone ringing on the other end of the line.

"Hello?" a voice answered.

"Yes," Jack said. "May I please speak to Mr. O'Connell?"

"This is Mr. O'Connell," a voice crackled through the tiny speaker.

"Well, sorry to bother you at home, sir," Jack went on, "but we've got a problem."

Mr. O'Connell listened patiently while Jack explained the story. When Jack had finished, Mr. O'Connell paused. "I didn't see anyone by the bench," he said, "but come to think of it, I did see Charlie Watts leave the game with a video. In fact, I asked him about it and Charlie told me it was a movie. . . . I forget the exact title. . . . *Fatal Globe* . . ."

"*Lethal Planet, Part Three*?" Bryan asked.

"That's it!" the scorekeeper exclaimed. "Anyway, Charlie said he was off to return the film."

"That's all you saw?" Lara asked.

"That's it, kids," Mr. O'Connell replied.

"Thanks for your help," Jack said.

"No problem."

Jack hung up and faced his friends. "Well, we know that Charlie was watching *Lethal Planet* yesterday. Maybe he was going to return it?"

"Maybe," Lara said. "And maybe not. But I say it's time we have a chat with Robin."

*　　　*　　　*

It was four in the afternoon by the time the gang reached Robin's front door and rang the bell.

"So this is where the competition lives," Bryan said.

"I wouldn't be surprised if she didn't let you in," Sam said. "She'd probably be scared that you'd steal some of her secrets."

"Hey, I don't steal," Bryan said. "I'm always completely original. I wouldn't even steal from Hitchcock or Spielberg."

The door opened and Robin poked her head out. Her curly blond hair was pulled back with a red baby doll hair clip.

"Hi, Bryan," she greeted him. "Come to steal from me?"

"No way," Bryan said. "Never."

"Then what are you guys doing here?" she asked.

"Aren't you going to invite us in?" Jack asked.

"Sorry," Robin said, quickly. "I can't. I'm in the middle of something."

"What?" Bryan asked.

"You're the last person I'd tell," Robin replied with a smile. "But if you must know, it has to do with my documentary. I'm planning this week's shooting schedule."

"Well, we won't keep you then," Lara said. "We just wanted to ask you a few quick questions."

"Okay, shoot," Robin replied.

"What were you doing at our game today with a video camera?" Lara asked.

"That's easy," Robin replied. "I was working on my film."

"What were you doing by our bench during halftime?" Jack asked.

Robin blinked. "Your bench? I didn't know I was even near your bench."

"All right," Bryan said. "But why were you filming at our game? Does your project relate to basketball?"

Robin batted her eyes and smiled. "Who knows?"

"Aw, come on," Bryan said. "We're on a case and trying to get some information.

I'm not trying to steal your *precious* ideas."

"I want to win that prize just as much as you," Robin shot back. "I'd kill for a chance to hang out at the news station for a week. I don't mean to be a jerk, but sorry. I'm not saying anything more. You'll find out about my film next week when I collect the grand prize. Now, if you guys will excuse me, I'm behind schedule."

She slammed the door shut.

"She sure told us," Bryan said sheepishly.

A half hour later the gang sat in Jack's living room. After getting permission from his parents, he had invited everyone over for dinner, which was almost ready.

"She's so guilty!" Jack exclaimed.

"I think so, too," Corey said.

"But we don't have any hard-core proof," Lara noted. "Just because someone is a little rude and mysterious doesn't make that person a crook."

"And don't forget that we saw Charlie trip Ray Washington on the tape, and Sam saw him trip Lara at the game," Bryan said. "I still say he's our man."

Lara sighed. "But we don't have any proof about him either. Our evidence is circumstantial. It's our word against his."

Bryan held up the switched video. "All we've got is a bunch of migrating caribou. Some evidence!"

"Hey," Jack said. "Let me see that a minute."

"This tape?" Bryan asked. "Why?"

"I'm interested in caribou," Jack replied. "Come on. Please." He held out his hand.

Bryan shrugged, and said, "Here you go." Then he tossed the tape across the room.

Jack got up from the sofa and slipped the tape in the VCR. "We never did watch the whole tape," he said. "Maybe there's something we missed."

"There's nothing useful on that," Sam said. "You think someone would be dumb enough to switch the tape but leave a major clue on it?"

"You never know," Lara said. "In most of the spy books I've read, the crook gives himself away with something obvious—something so obvious that it's easy to overlook. That's why detectives have got to be thorough."

"My thoughts exactly," Jack said. "You guys can keep talking but I'm looking for clues."

"All right, all right," Bryan said. "But put it on fast forward so we can watch those herds really move."

And for the next five minutes that's exactly what the Sonics did.

"Nothing," Corey said as the animals whipped across the screen.

"Probably," Jack admitted. "But hold on, we're almost near the end. A few more minutes . . . wait! Did you see that?"

"See what?" Sam asked lazily.

Jack rewound. "My eagle eyes caught something again."

He pressed play, this time at regular

speed. The gang gathered around the TV.

"It's coming up soon," Jack said, as a shot of a single caribou at a watering hole came on the screen. "It's short but it's there."

"Wake me when this is over," Bryan said from the couch. He closed his eyes.

"Look!" Jack shouted.

"I saw something!" Lara said. "It looked like a group of people."

Bryan sat up on the couch. "Let's see it again."

Jack rewound the tape and pressed play. Once again, the lone caribou came on screen. An instant later the animal was replaced by a picture of . . . Superman? And then a clown and a ghost? Then suddenly the caribou was back on screen, drinking out of a pool of muddy water.

"What in the world was that?" Corey asked.

"It looks like a costume party or something," Lara said.

"A Halloween party!" Bryan said, snapping his fingers. "And I know whose film it was!"

"Whose?" Lara asked.

Bryan's eyes were bright. "We've got our crook," he announced, triumphantly. "You see, Robin's film in last year's contest was a documentary on a Halloween party! Don't you guys get it? She used a copy of one of her old films as the switched tape. But she forgot to erase every bit of it. I say we pay her another visit after dinner."

"Sounds good to me," Lara said. "Although it's hard to believe that someone as skilled with videotape as Robin would make such a careless mistake."

"You said yourself that the smartest crooks often do stupid things," Sam said.

"I did say that," Lara agreed. "Robin seems to be the culprit."

Just then, Jack's mother stuck her head in the living room. "Dinner anyone?"

Jack looked at his hungry friends, who all smiled. "You bet!" he said.

ROBIN HELPS

Lara and the gang wolfed down their food, anxious to get to Robin's and solve the case.

"Wait a second, kids," Jack's mother said when they were done eating. "Don't you have homework? It's Sunday and you all have school tomorrow."

"We've done it already, Mrs. Cummings," Lara said. "And we only need to visit Robin for a few minutes."

"Right, Mom," Jack said. "We've got a case to crack."

Jack's mother sighed. "How is it that

81

five ordinary children always seem to get involved with solving mysteries?"

"Just lucky, I guess," Sam said.

"Oh, okay," Jack's mother said. "But all of you—call home for permission first."

One by one, Lara, Corey, Bryan, and Sam called home. Fifteen minutes later, they were walking down the block back to Robin's house.

Jack rubbed his hands together as he stood on Robin's doorstep. "Boy, is she going to be surprised to see us," he said.

"I can't wait to see her break down and beg for mercy," Bryan added.

But Lara wasn't as sure as her friends. Although the evidence pointed to Robin, Lara still had her doubts. It wasn't based on anything concrete, just a gut feeling that there were still layers of this mystery left to be uncovered.

Robin opened the front door. She wore a bright purple baby doll clip in her blond hair.

"You guys again?" she asked with a smile. "Some people just don't know when to give up."

Lara wanted to control the questioning, but Jack and Bryan started talking before she could speak.

"You switched Bryan's video," Jack blurted. "We've got proof."

"I did *what*?" Robin asked.

"And you turned off my camera during halftime today," Bryan added.

"Are you guys nuts?" Robin asked. "What are you talking about?"

"That you're a no good—" Jack began.

"Hey!" Lara interrupted. She turned to Robin. "Can we come in and discuss this? It won't take long but we need some questions answered."

Robin sighed. "Oh, all right."

She swung the door open. Lara noticed three video cameras in the living room. The dining room table was being used as an editing board.

"Wow," Lara heard Bryan mutter. "And I thought *I* was into making videos."

"So what's the problem?" Robin asked. "Why don't you start at the beginning."

"Good idea," Corey said, and with help from the rest of the gang, she brought Robin up-to-date, carefully explaining every bit of evidence.

When Corey was through, Lara saw Robin shake her head and begin to smile. Soon the smile grew into a grin and a second later she was laughing.

"She thinks it's a big joke," Bryan said. He turned to Robin. "I've got news for you, Robin. Sabotaging my film isn't funny!"

"I haven't done a thing to your film," Robin snapped.

Bryan took a step back. "You haven't?"

"No!" Robin stated. "And I can prove it."

Lara wrinkled her brow. Perhaps her detective intuition had been right. "You can?" she asked. "How?"

"Wait here," Robin said.

With those words, she disappeared down a staircase.

"Think she's trying to cut out the back?" Jack asked, after a pause.

"I doubt it," Corey said. "She knows we'd find her again. This *is* her house."

A few seconds later, Lara heard footsteps returning.

"Here," Robin said, entering the room and tossing a video on the sofa. "That is my one and only copy of my Halloween documentary from last year. Go ahead and look at it if you want."

Jack picked up the tape and read the side label out loud: "'All Hallow's Eve: A Documentary.'"

"So what?" Bryan asked. "What does that prove?"

"Don't you see?' Robin asked. "It isn't *my* copy of the Halloween film that was covered up by caribou."

"But if it isn't yours . . . whose is it?" Sam asked.

"The party was at Marianne Watts's house," Robin said. "When I finished the film I made a copy for her. There shouldn't be any other copies in existence."

Lara blinked. "You mean, Marianne—Charlie's sister?"

"Right," Robin said. "Marianne's my best friend."

"So maybe Charlie *did* do it," Jack said.

"Maybe," Lara agreed. She turned to Robin. "But how do you explain the orange baby doll hair clip we found under our bench?"

All the Sonics stared at the bright purple clip in Robin's hair.

"Who knows?" Robin said. "Lots of people wear hair clips."

"But every time I've seen you, you've been wearing a different color one," Sam said. "Yesterday it was pink, and earlier today it was red."

"And I lost an orange one a couple of days ago," Robin explained.

"Where'd you lose it?" Lara asked.

Robin shrugged. "If I knew, I'd find it."

"That sounds like an easy explanation to me," Jack stated.

"Too easy," Bryan agreed. "You must

have some idea where you lost it."

"Come to think of it," Robin said slowly, "I was at Marianne's two days ago and then I couldn't find it that evening. That's all I can remember."

The gang was silent for a moment. Aside from the obvious hair clip clue, Lara wondered about something else. "Robin," she asked, "can you tell us what you were doing by our bench this afternoon? Look at it from our point of view. Your actions seem pretty suspicious."

"Try *extremely* suspicious!" Jack stated.

"Isn't there anything I can do to clear my name?" Robin asked sadly. She shook her head and sat down on the sofa.

"Are you all right?" Corey asked.

"I'm fine," Robin said. She glared at the gang. "But I'm *not* a thief." And then, much to the Sonics' surprise, she reached for the phone.

"Calling the police?" Jack asked.

"No," Robin said, "Marianne."

Moments later, Lara heard Robin speak into the receiver. "Hi, it's Robin. Listen . . . I'm in trouble. The Sonics think I'm stealing their videotapes. This is kind of strange, but it's possible that Charlie has been tripping people during games. Maybe he's behind all of this. What? He's not home?"

Robin looked up. "Charlie's at BigTime Video," she said.

Lara saw Bryan narrow his eyes. Then he nodded while Robin spoke into the phone again. "That'd be great, Marianne. Thanks!"

Robin hung up. "Okay," she said, facing the gang. "We haven't got long, but Marianne said we were welcome to look around her house. Maybe Charlie has the switched tape in his room."

"All right, then," Lara said. "Onward to Charlie's." She turned to Bryan. "Did you think of something?"

The redhead nodded. "I sure did. The initials on the switched tape were BTV.

That's BigTime Video. That's where Charlie says he buys all of his tapes."

"More importantly," Robin said, "that's also where *I* buy all my tapes. If Charlie did pull the switch using Marianne's copy of my Halloween party film, the switched tape is one that *I* bought."

"This doesn't look good for Charlie," Corey said.

"You said it," Sam agreed. "Let's hustle. Charlie'll get home soon. We haven't got much time!"

8

THE SEARCH

A little while later, Robin and the Sonics stood on Charlie's doorstep. Jack rang the bell and Marianne opened the door.

"So," Marianne said to Robin, "are these the guys who are trying to throw you in jail?"

"Not jail," Lara said. "Just trying to get to the bottom of this mystery."

"Well, you'd better hurry," Marianne said. "Charlie will be home any minute."

"One quick question first," Sam said. "How many copies of Robin's Halloween party video are there?"

Robin shot Sam a glance. "I told you, two," she said angrily.

"Just making sure," Sam said. He turned to Marianne. "Well?"

"Just like Robin said," Marianne replied. "There are only two."

"Have you seen yours lately?" Lara asked Marianne. "Please. It could be important."

"I'll tell you what," Marianne said. "You go on up and check Charlie's room. I'll see if I can find my copy of the Halloween documentary in the basement. Go ahead. Up the stairs, first room on your right."

The Sonics didn't need any more prompting. Corey bounded up the stairs, followed by her friends and Robin. They walked down a short hallway, and then Corey pushed Charlie's door open.

Charlie's room had posters of the Minnesota Twins, the Minnesota Timberwolves, and a school pennant hanging on the walls. A football sat on the windowsill. To the left was a desk with a computer, and next to that was a bookshelf.

"There are six of us," Sam said. "We should be able to check this place out pretty fast. Let's get to work."

Corey looked over the desk, Lara checked around the window, Bryan and Jack inspected the closets, and Sam checked under the bed while Robin looked behind the bookshelf.

"Anyone find anything?" Corey called out after a minute.

"Just some old socks," Sam said.

"And an overdue library book," Robin said from the bookshelf.

"I feel kind of bad about snooping through Charlie's things," Corey said.

"Remember, he *did* trip Lara," Bryan reminded her.

"Keep looking," Lara said.

Suddenly, the door burst open. Corey gasped, frightened for a moment that it was Charlie.

"I can't find my copy of the Halloween video," Marianne said. "You guys might be right—maybe Charlie did use it."

The Sonics smiled at each other. They could taste victory.

"It's got to be here somewhere," Bryan said. "Let's keep searching."

"Wait!" Corey said.

Everybody in the room froze.

"What?" Sam hissed.

"Shhh!" Corey said. "Listen!"

The sound of a door slamming shut echoed through the house!

"It's Charlie," Marianne whispered. "If he finds out that I let you in his room, he'll kill me. Remember how angry he got when he found me reading his journal, Robin?"

"I remember," Robin replied. "You had to sleep over at my house for a whole weekend."

"If he finds you guys here I'll have to move out!" Marianne cried. "You'd better find something—now!"

"We need more time!" Lara said. "Stall him downstairs!"

"How?" Marianne wailed.

"Just do it," Robin blurted. "If something goes wrong I'll take the blame— you can tell him it was all my fault."

Marianne smiled. "Thanks," she said and slipped out the door. Corey's heart was beating like mad.

"Come on," Bryan said, turning back to the closet. "Let's keep looking."

Corey opened the middle desk drawer. It was filled with assorted buttons, baseball cards, ticket stubs, and sheets of notebook paper. *Why are boys so messy?* she wondered as she dug her hands into the mess.

But wait . . . what was this? Corey's eyes went wide. Under a sheaf of papers she discovered at least twenty bottle caps—all for grape drink.

"Hey, guys," she exclaimed. "Look!"

Seconds later, the Sonics and Robin had gathered around her.

"What's so great about grape drink?" Robin asked.

"It's a clue we found earlier," Lara explained. "Good work, Corey."

"Don't thank me," Corey said, as the gang went back to their search. "Let's just be thankful that Charlie keeps so much junk!"

"Let's not celebrate yet," Bryan said. "We still need that tape or else we can't prove a thing."

"You mean this tape?" Corey heard Jack ask.

"Let's see it," Bryan asked.

Jack tossed the videotape to Bryan, who caught it and quickly shook his head. "This says BTV on the side. I get my tapes at Power Video. Look for a PV on the side."

Jack sighed and returned to searching.

Corey turned back to the desk. *We've got to find that tape,* she thought. *Charlie will be up here any minute!*

But just as Corey was reaching for the bottom drawer of the desk, she heard something that gave her goose bumps: footsteps on the stairs! Charlie was on his way up!

The Sonics exchanged a worried glance.

"Keep looking!" Lara mouthed.

Her heart thumping, Corey turned back to the desk. Then she gasped—she heard Charlie's voice right outside the door!

"What's wrong with you, Marianne?" Charlie said. "Leave me alone."

"Aw, come on, Charlie," Corey heard Marianne say. "I want to show you this picture I made. It's downstairs."

"All right," Charlie said. "But in a minute. I want to dump my stuff in my room."

"No, Charlie," Marianne begged. "Now."

Corey looked over her shoulder. Lara, Bryan, Jack, and Robin were frozen in place, listening to the conversation in the hallway. Sam was peeking under the bed.

"Marianne, you're being so weird!" Charlie exclaimed.

"Please, Charlie," Marianne said.

Suddenly, Sam called out, "I got it!"

Corey looked across the room. Sam

was holding a tape in his hands—but was it the right one?

The door swung open. Corey wheeled around. Charlie stood in the doorway, his eyes wide with surprise.

"What's going on here?" he demanded.

"We were looking for this!" Sam said, holding the tape over his head. "And we found it!"

Even from across the room Corey could see that the tape Sam held in his hands had the initials "PV" on it. She breathed a sigh of relief.

"What the—?" Charlie began. "This is trespassing. Get out of my room! Marianne—how could you have let these guys in my room?"

For the next few moments, everyone was talking at once. Sam, Jack, and Bryan accused Charlie of cheating and Charlie denied it and demanded that they leave his room.

"I'll report you to Mr. Crimmins!" Charlie cried.

"No, we'll report you!" Sam countered.

"Whoa!" Lara exclaimed. "Let's settle down." She turned to Charlie. "Maybe if we explain things you'll understand why we're here."

"You'd better," Charlie said, folding his arms across his chest. "And make it fast."

"Okay, everyone," Lara said. "Take a seat."

For the next five minutes Corey and the gang listened to Lara present the evidence: the grape drink, the switched tape, and the Halloween party.

"So you see," Lara said, holding up the tape Sam had found under Charlie's bed, "if this tape is Bryan's, you're in big trouble."

Everybody in the room was silent. Charlie sat on his bed and looked at his feet. Corey could hear the wind blowing through the trees outside.

"Okay," Charlie whispered finally. "I'm guilty."

He looked up at the gang sadly. "I

guess I want to win too badly sometimes. I don't mean to hurt anyone, but then in the heat of the game I go nuts . . . I sort of lose it."

"I'll say," Sam said.

Charlie looked to Lara. "I've felt awful about your ankle all day."

"Right," Lara said. "Just like you felt bad about Ray Washington yesterday."

Charlie looked back at the floor, his face red.

"Let's head over to Mr. Crimmins's house," Bryan said. "We want a rematch."

"Before we go, there's still one more thing that doesn't add up," Lara said.

"What?" Robin asked.

"How your orange baby doll hair clip got under our bench," Lara told Robin.

Charlie wiped his eyes and looked up. "I think I can explain."

"Go ahead," Corey prompted him.

"Well," Charlie began. "I found it in our hallway—"

"I told you I lost it," Robin told Bryan.

"I believe you now," Bryan said.

"I was going to give it back to you," Charlie said to Robin, "but when I saw Bryan's film bag, I had to use something to make them think someone else switched the tape."

"So you tried to frame my best friend?" Marianne asked.

Once again, Charlie collapsed on the bed. Corey had never seen someone look so low.

"Yeah," he said softly. He looked up at Robin. "I guess I've got to stop caring so much about winning."

"That's for sure," Lara said.

"Speaking of winning," Robin said to Bryan, "I'm sorry I've been so competitive with you over the video prize." She put out her hand. "May the best video win."

Bryan took Robin's hand and shook it. "Sounds good to me," he said with a smile. "Who knows? After all of this it would be pretty funny if someone else won the contest."

Robin laughed. "That would certainly serve us right."

REMATCH

Bryan hustled out of his mother's car into the community center. It was a week later, the day of the Sonics' rematch against the Smashers.

He burst into the boys' locker room. "Is Lara going to be able to play?" he asked.

Mr. Lester stood by a sink, punching numbers into his calculator. "According to my figures," he said with a smile, "the answer is a definite yes."

"All right!" Bryan cried.

All week long, Lara had rested her

sore ankle in hopes of being ready to take on the Smashers again.

"She's already on the court practicing her shot with the rest of the team," Jack called from his locker.

"Is she sinking them like last week?" Bryan asked.

"I don't know yet," Jack replied. "But I'm on my way now. See you there!"

Bryan planted himself by a locker and began to change. As he laced up his sneakers, Mr. Lester sat next to him, looking strangely serious.

"Well, Bryan," the coach said, "I was sorry to hear about your video."

Bryan blinked. "Oh, yeah," he said. "That was tough luck."

"You must remember," Mr. Lester went on, "that second place isn't so bad. I've done extensive research on the likelihood of placing first in a competition two years in a row. I'm afraid the chances of repeating are only twenty-five percent."

Bryan nodded. "Maybe I was a little

overconfident. I saw Robin's film and I think she beat me fair and square."

"That's a good sportsmanlike attitude," Mr. Lester said with a nod. "Now finish getting changed and I'll see you on the court."

After the coach had left, Bryan put on his Sonics uniform and then reached into his gym bag for his sneakers. But instead of brushing against leather like he was expecting, Bryan's hand hit something metallic. He smiled and pulled a bronze plaque out of the bag.

Great, he thought. *My second place prize. Another plaque.*

With a sigh, Bryan put the award back in his bag, laced his sneakers, and headed out to the court.

A large crowd was already waiting in the stands. Bryan saw Mr. Hanraddy sitting in his customary spot: front row behind the Sonics' bench. The old man waved a pennant and gave Bryan the thumbs-up sign.

"You can do it, Bryan!" he cried.

"Tough defense! That's the ticket!"

Bryan smiled and joined his teammates at the opposite end of the court for some layup drills.

"Hey!" Sam called. He fired Bryan the ball.

Bryan took the pass and tossed the ball into the basket.

"Two points!" Corey cried.

Bryan got his own rebound and fired a pass to Lara. She dribbled twice, took aim, and shot.

"Swish!" Jack said.

"She hasn't lost a thing!" Sam said. "The Smashers are goners!"

Lara grinned. "We're going to win," she said. "I can feel it."

Bryan saw her look to the opposite end of the court where the Smashers were warming up. The team was exactly the same as the week before—but without Charlie, who had been suspended from all league sports for a year. Bryan had also heard through the grapevine that Charlie's parents had denied him video privileges for the rest of the school year. A tough punishment, but one Bryan thought he deserved. Even so, Bryan would miss Charlie's dynamic moves on the court—as long as he didn't have to play against him!

Just then, Bryan heard a whistle pierce the air. He looked up to see Mr. Crimmins at midcourt, waving his arms. "Alright, boys and girls," the referee called. "Let's get this show on the road."

Bryan thought back to the previous Monday. He and the other members of the Sonics had knocked on Mr. Crimmins's door and presented him with the real tape along with a written confession from Charlie.

"This is a sad day for Ridgefield County sports," the referee had said with a shake of his head. "A sad day indeed."

But Mr. Crimmins had done what he felt was right. He had contacted the league and Charlie's parents. Bryan tried to block the memory out and concentrate on the game.

"Go, Sonics!" Mr. Hanraddy called from the stands.

Bryan looked up. Sitting behind Mr. Hanraddy were Robin and Marianne. Bryan waved. He had seen Robin the night before at the junior filmmaker awards dinner. It had been tough to sit there and watch Robin win that weeklong internship at WBGA, but like he had told Mr. Lester, he had to admit that Robin's film was better.

"All right, team," Mr. Lester said as Bryan headed back to the bench. "Just because Charlie is out doesn't mean we're not going to have to play solid basketball. Lots of teams have lost their star player only to regroup and win."

"Right," Sam said. "Don't forget when Willis Reed of the Knicks got hurt in game five of the 1969 Championship."

"How can we forget," Bryan asked,

"when that's all you talk about?"

"I was just trying to spice up things with a little history," Sam said with a grin.

The buzzer sounded.

"Okay, Sonics!" Mr. Lester cried. "Go out there and defy the odds!"

Bryan threw his towel on the bench and headed for center court where John Willows was waiting for him.

Bryan slapped the opposing center's hand. "Good luck," he said.

"You too," John replied.

Bryan saw his teammates slap hands all around. Then Mr. Crimmins dribbled the ball twice and blew his whistle. "Let's have a good clean game, kids."

The referee tossed the opening jump ball. Bryan was ready, and leaped high, tapping the ball to Lara. Lara passed it to Jack who easily avoided the boy trying to cover him. Bryan jogged down-court and posted up near the basket. Jack saw him and fired a pass. Bryan turned and shot.

"Swish!" Sam called.

Bryan raised his arms in the air. He may have lost the filmmaking prize but he hadn't lost his inside game.

"Don't get cocky now, Bryan," he heard Mr. Hanraddy call. "Let's play some defense!"

Bryan looked up to see John Willows out ahead of him on a fast break. Bryan sprinted downcourt, but he was too late—a long outlet pass soared over his head into John's hands. John dribbled twice, and then sank an easy layup. Bryan saw Mr. Lester shake his head and punch numbers into his calculator.

"Be careful of that," Sam called to Bryan.

Bryan nodded. "I will."

With Charlie out of the lineup, Jack had a much easier time bringing the ball upcourt. A few dribbles past half-court he saw Lara on the right wing and bounced a pass her way. Lara took a step behind the three-point line and fired. The ball arced through the air and dropped straight through the net.

The crowd cheered wildly.

"She's still got it!" Sam cried.

"Three points!" Mr. Crimmins yelled to the scorekeeper.

"This game is in the bag," Bryan cheered.

But Bryan might have spoken too soon. The same way he had misjudged Robin's competition in film-making, the Sonics found it hard to sustain a solid effort against the Smasher team. At halftime they led by only four points.

"You're playing like you've already got it won," Mr. Lester told them in the locker room. "Basketball is a game of emotion. You have to want it to win it."

Bryan and the other Sonics nodded. They would play all out. "No mercy!" Bryan yelled.

The rest of the Sonics took up his chant. "No mercy!" they all replied.

Yet the second half started horribly. The Smashers scored ten points in the first two minutes without the Sonics getting a single basket. After Smasher Brenda Frazier nailed another three-point shot, Mr. Lester signaled for a time-out. It was the first time Bryan had seen his coach truly angry.

"Are you guys going to play defense or what?" Mr. Lester cried, rubbing a hand over his bald head. "The Smashers aren't going to dry up and blow away. They came to play!"

"Wow," Bryan whispered to Lara as they headed out to the court. "He was mad!"

"He sure was," Lara agreed. "He didn't even reach for his calculator!"

Mr. Lester's outburst was exactly what the gang needed to spur them into action. The next time down the court, Jack sent a low pass to Bryan. Bryan felt John Willows right behind him and passed the ball to Corey. She fired the ball to Sam, who was cutting to the hoop. Sam pulled up and nailed a five-footer.

"That's the way!" Mr. Lester called. "Now get back! Get back!"

Next time down the court, Bryan blocked a shot. Jack grabbed the loose ball and fired it to Corey, who sank the ball for another two points.

"That's the way to get back in it!" Mr. Hanraddy called.

Bryan smiled. He saw Robin give him the thumbs-up. Next time down the court, Brenda Frazier missed on a drive to the hoop. Bryan, suddenly filled with confidence, boxed out, grabbed the rebound, and fired an outlet pass to Corey. She passed the ball to Sam, who fired a behind-the-back pass to Lara. Lara calmly took a shot.

Score!

Bryan smiled. Now they were playing. The buzzer sounded with the Sonics up by five, heading into the fourth quarter.

"Keep playing aggressively," Mr. Lester said on the sidelines. "Pass the ball. Good ball movement leads to open shots. Concentrate."

And the Sonics did. For the next eight minutes they played the best basketball of the season. They hit the open man, boxed out for rebounds, and dove for loose balls. With a couple of minutes to go, Mr. Lester cleared the bench, giving Joe Tanksley, Peter Fisk, and Marla Armstrong a chance to get some time on the court. The game was in the bag. When the final buzzer sounded, the scoreboard read: Sonics 68, Smashers 51.

"Nice game," Mr. Lester said to Bryan, shaking his hand.

"Thanks!" Bryan yelled.

He whooped loudly and ran to mid-court to celebrate. Soon the court was jammed with players and onlookers. After shaking hands with the Smashers, Bryan felt a tap on his shoulder.

"Bryan," Robin said. "Good game."

Bryan nodded. "Thanks," he said. "And Robin, you know I never told you . . . but your video was great. It was a terrific idea to do a documentary on how recycling saves the environment. Congratulations."

Robin seemed almost embarrassed. "Well, I knew I'd have to work hard to beat you."

Bryan felt himself blush.

"Anyway," Robin went on, "I don't think the people at WBGA would mind if I brought a visitor with me one day. Are you interested?"

Bryan smiled broadly. "You bet!"

As Robin disappeared into the crowd, Bryan whooped as loudly as he could. He found Corey, Sam, Lara, and Jack at midcourt.

"What do you say we get some ice cream?" Sam suggested.

"Great idea," Jack replied. "Then maybe we can go over to my place to watch a video?"

"Fine," Bryan said, laughing. "Under one condition."

"What's that?" Corey asked.

Bryan grinned widely. "No caribou."

The gang laughed.

"How about *Lethal Planet, Part Four?*" Sam suggested.

"Now, you're talking," Bryan exclaimed. "That's the perfect way to celebrate a championship!"